BAT JAMBOREE

by **Kathi Appelt**

illustrated by **Melissa Sweet**

Scholastic Inc.

New York   Toronto   London   Auckland   Sydney

To Donna, who believes
—K.A.

To my friend Nina
—M.S.

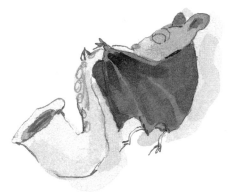

ISBN 0-590-76767-4

12 11 10 9 8 7 6 5 4 3 2 1   7 8 9/9 0 1 2/0

Printed in the U.S.A.   08

First Scholastic printing, September 1997

The Bat Jamboree
was held early this year
at the old drive-in movie
not too far from here.

It starred 55 bats
who had practiced all spring
for this grandest of shows
on the old silver screen.

The program was better
than ever before.
It was standing room only,
no more seats on the floor.

The crowd settled in
as the houselights went down.
The spotlight came up.
There wasn't a sound.

Then…

1 bat sang.

2 bats flapped.

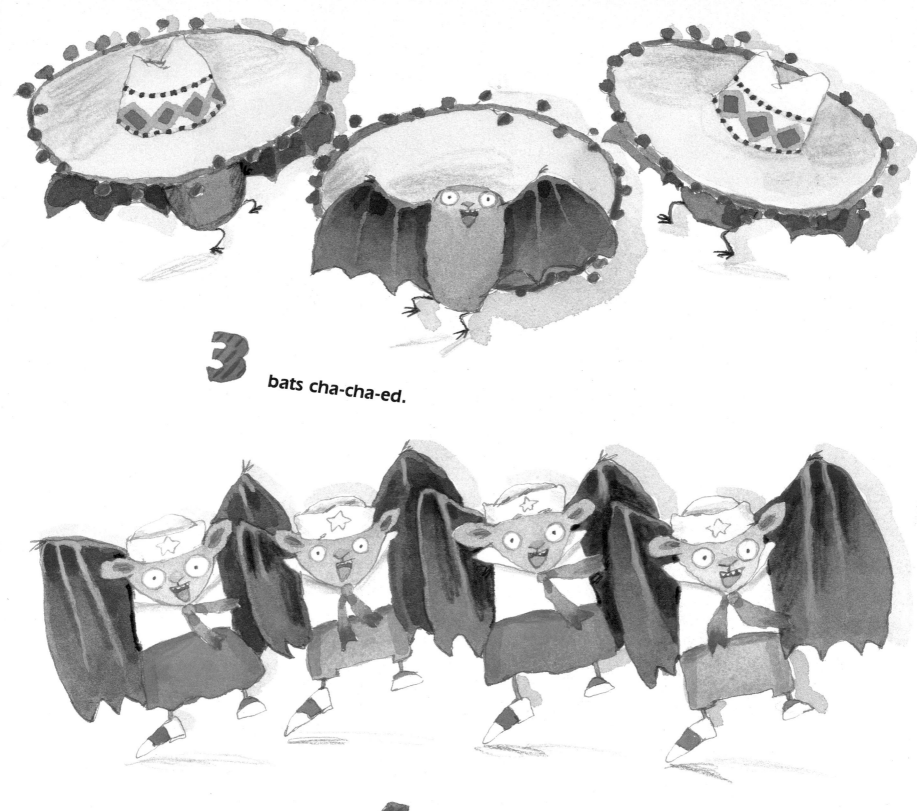

3 bats cha-cha-ed.

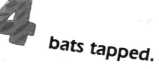

4 bats tapped.

5 bats dove from the top of the screen,
reeling and whirling wing tip to wing.

6 bats formed the band, oh, how they jived.
Their instruments wailed in three-quarter time.

7 bats balanced 7 balls on their noses.

8 bats doubled up and danced Cotton-Eyed Joeses.

9 bats wore tuxedos and sang in a chorus.
Each thought to himself: How they adore us!

The time came, at last, for the grand finale:
The Acro-Bats!

Yes, there were **10** bats in all-e.
They strutted in front of the six-story screen
in a dazzling display of bats on the wing.

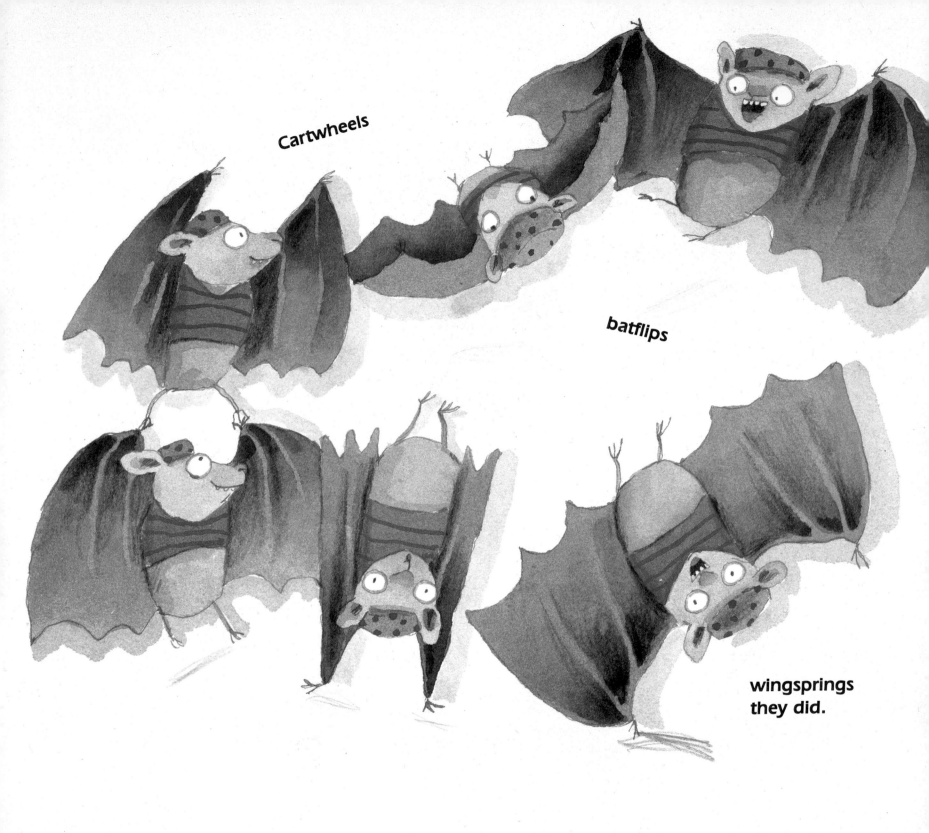

Cartwheels

batflips

wingsprings
they did.

But the greatest of all was...

The Great Bat Pyramid.
It started, you see, with the Acro-Bats
all lined up in a row...then,
yes, and then...

10

9 bats fluttered.

8 bats flew.

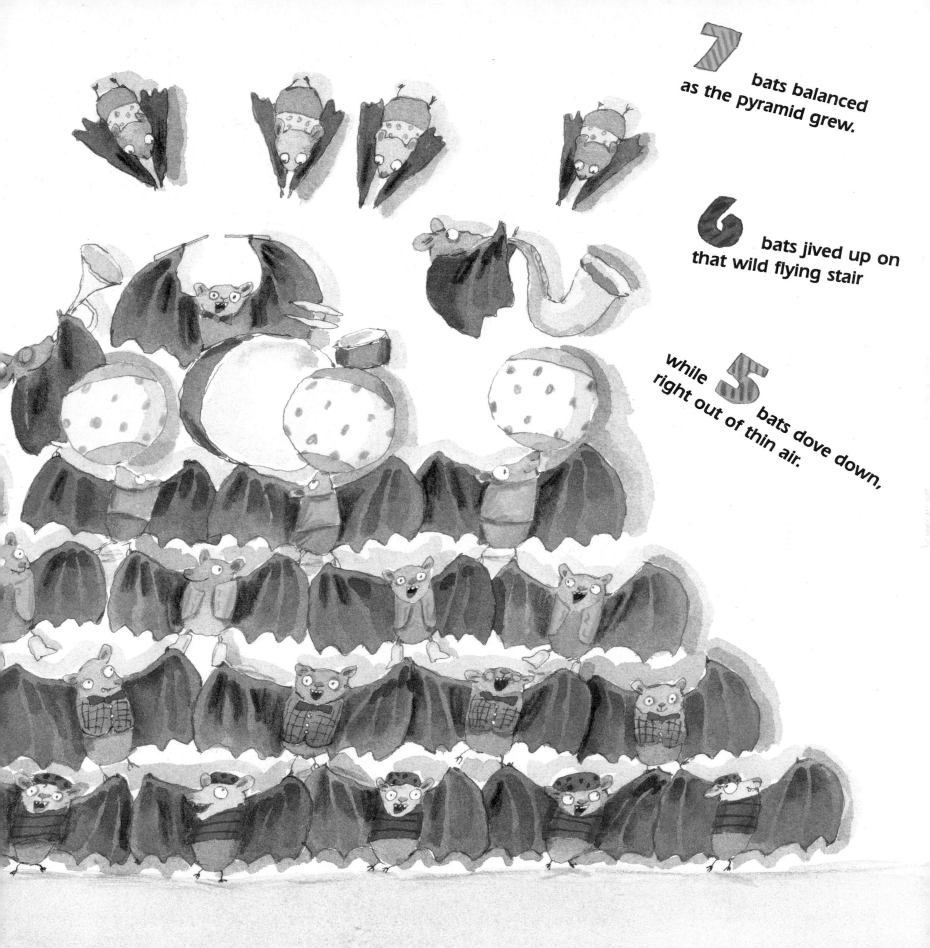

7 bats balanced as the pyramid grew.

6 bats jived up on that wild flying stair

while **5** bats dove down, right out of thin air.

4 bats tapped
as they all 4 ascended.

And up **3** bats cha-cha-ed,
fandangoed, and twisted.

When **2** bats flapped up
the crowd became quiet.
They'd never seen anything,
anything like it.

Now 54 bats
in that wonderful band
all waited in silence
for
        the 1

                bat
                    to
                        land.
No one moved a muscle
as she flew to the peak,
not even a whisper,
not even a squeak.
And it seemed like forever—
the tension it grew—
to the top of the pyramid
the bat lady flew.

And once up on top,
in a voice all aquiver,
the single bat sang,
making all the bats shiver.

The whole crowd went crazy.
They hooted, they howled,
as all 55 bats took a deep bow.

And then it was over:
The spotlight was dimmed,
the houselights came up,
the curtains were trimmed.

But come again next year
and the one after that
for the Bat Jamboree
starring 55 bats.

The spotlight will shine
on that six-story screen.
And the show won't be over
till the bat lady sings.